P9-AFZ-870

In a high-rise building
deep in the heart of a big city
live two private eyes:
Bunny Brown and Jack Jones.
Bunny is the brains,
Jack is the snoop,
and together they
crack cases wide open.

This is the story of
Case Number 007:
THE CASE OF
THE BAFFLED BEAR.

story by
Cynthia Rylant

pictures by
G. Brian Karas

THE
HIGH-RISE

PRIVATE
EYES

The High-Rise Private Eyes

The Case of the
Baffled Bear

WITHDRAWN

HarperCollinsPublishers

Acrylic, gouache, and pencil were used for the full-color art.
The text type is Times.

HarperCollins®, 🐛®, and I Can Read Book®
are trademarks of HarperCollins Publishers Inc.

The High-Rise Private Eyes: The Case of the Baffled Bear
Text copyright © 2004 by Cynthia Rylant
Illustrations copyright © 2004 by G. Brian Karas
Manufactured in China.
For information address HarperCollins Children's Books,
a division of HarperCollins Publishers,
10 East 53rd Street, New York, NY 10022.
www.harperchildrens.com

Library of Congress Cataloging-in-Publication Data

Rylant, Cynthia.
The high-rise private eyes: the case of the baffled bear /
story by Cynthia Rylant ; pictures by G. Brian Karas.
    p.   cm. — (The high-rise private eyes ; case no. 007)
"Greenwillow Books."
Summary: Bunny and Jack, animal detectives,
take a break from playing cards to look for
Bernard Bear's missing messenger whistle.
ISBN-13: 978-0-06-053448-6 (trade bdg.) — ISBN-10: 0-06-053448-6 (trade bdg.)
ISBN-13: 978-0-06-053449-3 (lib. bdg.) — ISBN-10: 0-06-053449-4 (lib. bdg.)
ISBN-13: 978-0-06-053450-9 (pbk.) — ISBN-10: 0-06-053450-8 (pbk.)
[1. Animals—Fiction. 2. Mystery and detective stories.]
I. Karas, G. Brian, ill. II. Title.
PZ7.R982Ca 2004   [E]—dc22   2003012567
                         11 12 13 SCP 10 9 8 7 6
                                   ❖
Originally published by Greenwillow Books, an imprint of HarperCollins Publishers, in 2004.

Contents

Chapter 1
Pretzels

Every Tuesday night Bunny and Jack

liked to play Slap Jack.

They played for pretzels.

It was Jack's idea

to play for pretzels.

It was Bunny's idea

to play Slap Jack.

She thought the name was funny.

Jack did not.

"Why couldn't they call it

Worship Jack?" he said.

"Or Adore Jack?

Or at least Feed Jack?"

"Don't worry, Jack," said Bunny.

"I won't slap you."

"Will you let me win?" asked Jack.

Bunny looked at the pile of pretzels

she had won.

"What do you think?" asked Bunny.

Jack looked at the pretzel

he had won.

"This is pathetic," said Jack.

"Bingo," said Bunny.

"Maybe I'd win if we played

for saltwater taffy,"

said Jack.

"I don't have any

saltwater taffy,"

said Bunny.

"Exactly," said Jack.

"I should run and buy some."

"You just don't want to see me
eat all the pretzels," said Bunny.
She took a pretzel.
"Like *this* one," she said,
taking a bite.
"And this one," she said.
"And this one.
And this one."

"Gotta run," said Jack.

"I'll be back with taffy."

"And this one," said Bunny.

"And this one."

Jack picked up his pretzel.

"Pathetic," said Jack.

"And this one," said Bunny.

"I shall return!"

called Jack as he left.

"I shall *rule!*"

"And this one," said Bunny.

Chapter 2
The Case

Jack returned with taffy and a bear.

"This is Bernard,"

Jack said to Bunny.

"And he is very, very, VERY upset."

Bernard nodded his head

and sniffled.

"Is he here to play cards?"

asked Bunny.

"Heavens, no!" said Jack.

"He is here to find his whistle."

16

Jack patted Bernard on the back.

"We have a case,"

Jack said proudly.

"Hmmm," said Bunny.

"Are you sure

this isn't about Slap Jack?"

"You slap Jack?"

asked Bernard, his eyes wide.

"Heavens, no!" said Jack.

"Bunny thinks I brought you here
because she was getting
all the pretzels."

"Excuse me?" said Bernard.

"But I'll *rule* with taffy,"
said Jack.

Bernard looked at Bunny.

"Maybe I should go," said Bernard.

"No, no," said Bunny. "I'm sorry.

We really do want to help.

We won't say anything else

about Slap Jack."

"You slap Jack?" asked Bernard.

"Ugh," said Bunny.

"She worships me," said Jack.

With a lot of taffy

and a lot of questions,

Bunny and Jack got Bernard's story.

"I'm a Speedy Messenger,"
said Bernard.

"We could sort of tell," said Jack.

"I've seen you guys
whiz through town on your bikes,"
said Bunny.

"That's why I need my whistle,"
said Bernard.

"To let everyone know
I'm coming through."

"Where exactly did you lose
this whistle?" asked Bunny.
She had her notepad and pencil ready.

"In the park, I think," said Bernard.
"I tried to whistle
at a dog on a scooter,
but suddenly my whistle
wasn't around my neck."

22

"What happened to the dog?"
asked Jack.

"I think he's still up that tree,"
said Bernard.

"Ooh," said Jack.

"A dog up a tree is not good."

"What color is the whistle?"

asked Bunny.

"It's red," said Bernard.

"It was on a silver chain."

"The chain must have broken

while you were riding

through the park," said Bunny.

Bernard hung his head.

"I can't believe it," he said.

"Speedy Messengers

never lose anything.

Now I've lost all my confidence."

"*And* your whistle," said Jack.

"But, hey, don't feel bad.

Everybody loses *something*

now and then."

"Like card games," said Bunny.

"I was thinking of socks," said Jack.

"I was thinking of Slap Jack,"
said Bunny.

Bunny and Jack looked at Bernard.

They waited.

"No comment," said Bernard.

"Let's head to the park,"

said Bunny.

Chapter 3
The Whistle

Bunny, Jack, and Bernard

walked through the park.

Bunny was looking for clues.

Bernard was sniffling.

And Jack was dodging kids on skates.

"Whoa!" said Jack.
"Whoa! Whoa!
These kids are going to
run me down," he told Bunny.
"We should find whistles
for *all* of them."
"Just be nimble, Jack,"
said Bunny.

Jack looked at Bunny.

Bunny looked at Jack.

"Tell me you're not going to say
anything about being quick,"
said Jack.

"Not a peep," said Bunny.

Bernard stopped
and looked at them both.

"Are all detectives like you?" he asked.

"Let's hope so!" said Jack.

"Okay," said Bunny. "*Clues*.
We have to look for clues."
"It's hard to look for clues
when it's so Spring-y outside,"
said Jack.

"The flowers are blooming,
the bees are buzzing,
the birds are singing."
"Concentrate, Jack,"
said Bunny.

33

"Just listen," said Jack.

"Listen to Spring."

Bunny sighed.

"Okay, okay. I'll listen

for *one minute*," she said.

Bernard and Bunny and Jack

listened for one minute.

They heard buzzing.

They heard singing.

They heard *whistling*.

"Hey!" said Bernard.

"That sounds like *my* whistle."

Everybody looked up.

At the top of a tall tree

sat a robin,

blowing *Bernard's whistle*!

"Hey!" yelled Bernard

at the robin.

"That's my whistle!"

Bunny looked at Jack.

"Why would a bird

blow a whistle?" she asked.

"Because he doesn't

have a trumpet?" said Jack.

Bernard looked at them both.

"We know," said Jack.

" 'No comment.' "

Chapter 4
Solved

With Bernard yelling at him,
the robin flew right down.
"I'm sorry!" he croaked.
"I'm sorry!"
The robin gave Bernard
the whistle and chain.

"I didn't know

who the whistle belonged to,"

croaked the robin.

Bunny looked at the bird.

"Do you need a drink of water?"

she asked.

"No, no," croaked the robin.

"I have laryngitis.

That's why I needed the whistle."

It turned out that the robin,
whose name was Frederico,
had just flown all the way
from Florida.

But during a freak snowstorm in Georgia
he had caught a cold.
And when he finally got to the park,
he had laryngitis.

"I couldn't make a sound.

So the other birds kept

knocking me out of my tree."

"Why?" asked Jack.

"Because a bird sings

to claim his territory,"

said Bunny.

"Right, Frederico?"

"Right," croaked Frederico.

"So you've been using my whistle
to stay in your tree?"
asked Bernard.
"Right," croaked Frederico.

Bernard looked at the robin.

He handed the bird the whistle.

"Keep it," said Bernard.

"Keep it?" croaked Frederico.

"Keep it until you can sing,"
said Bernard.

"Thank you," croaked Frederico.

"Thank you."

Jack looked at Bunny.

"Don't cry, Jack," said Bunny.

"But it's such a nice story,"

said Jack.

"Don't cry," said Bunny.

"He gave the bird his whistle,"

said Jack.

"Not a tear," said Bunny.

45

"If you don't cry,"

said Bernard,

"I'll give you a ride

on my bike."

"Really?" asked Jack.

"Can I deliver a message?"

"Sure," said Bernard.

"Groovy," said Jack.

"When you and Bernard get back,

we'll all play Slap Jack,"

said Bunny.

Frederico looked at Bunny.

"You slap Jack?" he croaked.

"Oh, for heaven's sake,"
said Bunny.